A Note to Parents and Caregivers:

Read-it! Readers are for children who are just starting on the amazing road to reading. These beautiful books support both the acquisition of reading skills and the love of books.

 The PURPLE LEVEL presents basic topics and objects using high frequency words and simple language patterns.

 The RED LEVEL presents familiar topics using common words and repeating sentence patterns.

 The BLUE LEVEL presents new ideas using a larger vocabulary and varied sentence structure.

 The YELLOW LEVEL presents more challenging ideas, a broad vocabulary, and wide variety in sentence structure.

 The GREEN LEVEL presents more complex ideas, an extended vocabulary range, and expanded language structures.

 The ORANGE LEVEL presents a wide range of ideas and concepts using challenging vocabulary and complex language structures.

When sharing a book with your child, read in short stretches, pausing often to talk about the pictures. Have your child turn the pages and point to the pictures and familiar words. And be sure to reread favorite stories or parts of stories.

There is no right or wrong way to share books with children. Find time to read with your child, and pass on the legacy of literacy.

Adria F. Klein, Ph.D.
Professor Emeritus
California State University
San Bernardino, California

Editor: Dodie Marie Miller
Page Production: Brandie Shoemaker
Art Director: Nathan Gassman
Associate Managing Editor: Christianne Jones

First American edition published in 2007 by
Picture Window Books
5115 Excelsior Boulevard
Suite 232
Minneapolis, MN 55416
877-845-8392
www.picturewindowbooks.com

Printed in the United States of America.

Library of Congress Cataloging-in-Publication Data
McAllister, Margaret (Margaret I.)
The magic porridge pot / by Margaret McAllister ; illustrated by Peter Utton.
p. cm. — (Read-it! readers)
Summary: When they give shelter to an old woman on a cold winter's night,
Mrs. Molly and the many children that share her home discover the next morning
that their guest has repaid their kindness by leaving them a very special pot.
ISBN-13: 978-1-4048-3122-3 (library binding)
ISBN-10: 1-4048-3122-3 (library binding)
[1. Magic—Fiction. 2. Pots—Fiction. 3. Food—Fiction.] I. Utton, Peter, ill. II. Title.
PZ7.M4782525Mag 2006
[E]—dc22   2006029137

The Magic Porridge Pot

by Margaret McAllister
illustrated by Peter Utton

Special thanks to our advisers for their expertise:

Adria F. Klein, Ph.D.
Professor Emeritus, California State University
San Bernardino, California

Susan Kesselring, M.A.
Literacy Educator
Rosemount–Apple Valley–Eagan (Minnesota) School District

PiCTURE WiNDOW BOOKS
Minneapolis, Minnesota

At the end of the village was Mrs. Molly's house. It had a big garden, and it was always full of children.

None of them were Mrs. Molly's own children. They had nobody else to look after them, so Mrs. Molly did.

Charlie was still a baby.

Pippa was nearly grown-up.

Paul and Jenny were in-between.

Mrs. Molly worried about Paul. He was small for his age, and he never spoke.

Mrs. Molly and the children grew carrots, cabbages, parsnips, potatoes, sprouts, spinach, and lots and lots and lots of lettuce. Mrs. Molly needed the vegetables to feed them all.

"The children must never go hungry," said Mrs. Molly. But sometimes it was hard to feed everyone.

One winter day, when the frost was as white as sugar and as hard as stone, Pippa went to the village.

When she came home, she was so cold that her face was pale and her nose was pink. Beside her was a very old woman carrying a bundle.

"I met her on the way home," said Pippa to Mrs. Molly. "She is on a long journey. She has nowhere to sleep tonight, so I brought her home."

"Good," said Mrs. Molly. "Bring her in to get warm."

Pippa took the old woman to sit by the warm stove. There was only soup for supper that night, but Mrs. Molly made sure that everyone had a share.

In the morning, when Mrs. Molly and the children got up, the old woman had gone. On the stove stood a large bowl with a lid on and a note:

This is the magic porridge pot.

It will never leave a child disappointed.

The children stood around the porridge pot.
Pippa held onto Charlie in case it was hot.
Mrs. Molly lifted the lid.
   "Ooh!" said Charlie.
   "I'm hungry!" said Jenny.
Paul said nothing, but his eyes looked very big.

The pot was full of steamy, creamy, hot, sweet porridge. It tasted like cream and honey. It made them feel warm inside. Everybody had second helpings.

Every morning in winter the pot was full of steamy, creamy porridge—that is, every morning except Jenny's birthday. That day, they found a cake with six candles in the porridge pot instead.

After the icy winter came the spring. Daffodils grew in the garden. The children woke up one morning and sniffed. A very nice smell was coming from the porridge pot.

"It smells warm," said Jenny.

"It smells like something that isn't porridge," said Pippa.

"Ooh!" said Charlie.
Paul said nothing at all.
"It smells like fresh bread," said Mrs. Molly.
She took off the lid. The smell was so
delicious that everyone felt hungry. Pippa
lifted Charlie up. Paul stood on tiptoe.

The pot was full of fresh, hot bread. There
was crusty bread, soft bread, brown bread,
and shiny white bread. There were curly rolls
and twisty rolls. There were rolls with sesame
seeds on top.

"It's time for breakfast," said Mrs. Molly.

All through the spring, the porridge pot made bread. It made crumpets, muffins, and cupcakes. On Sundays, it made sticky buns.

The days grew longer and longer and warmer and warmer. One morning, the sun rose and woke the birds. The birds sang and woke the children. The children all went with Mrs. Molly to look in the porridge pot.

"It's very cold," said Mrs. Molly as she took off the lid.

"It's pink and creamy," said Jenny.
"It's yogurt," said Pippa.
"Oh!" said Charlie.
Paul said nothing at all.
"Strawberry yogurt!" said Mrs. Molly.
"Bring your bowls!"

All summer, the porridge pot gave them thick, creamy yogurt. The yogurt came in strawberry, raspberry, banana, pineapple, blueberry, and lemon flavors.

Then, there was a chocolate cake on Pippa's birthday, and a birthday cake for Charlie with candy and two blue candles on top.

The days grew shorter and cooler. Birds gathered on the rooftops, ready to fly away. The leaves on the trees turned yellow.

One cold morning in October, Mrs. Molly took the lid off the porridge pot.

Paul said nothing, but his eyes looked enormous.

"Apple pie for breakfast!" said Mrs. Molly.

The next day, it was chicken pie. The day after that, there was blackberry pie, then vegetable pie.

The porridge pot made a different pie every day for two weeks.

Then it started again with apple pie. For Mrs. Molly's birthday, it made a cherry cake with nuts on top instead of candles. "It will be Paul's birthday next," said Mrs. Molly.

Paul nodded, but he said nothing.

Winter came again. There was frost on the
windows and ice on the path. One night, as the
children were going to bed, the snow began
to fall.

"I think the porridge pot will do something
new tomorrow," said Mrs. Molly. "I wonder
what it will be?"

Paul said nothing. But when they were all
tucked in bed, he could not sleep. Long ago,
when Paul was little, before he came to live with
Mrs. Molly, he was always hungry. There was
never enough to eat.

Paul could remember a day when he was very small and hungry. He had stood in the street and looked at a market stall full of fruit.

There were bananas like big yellow smiles and oranges like sunshine.

There were raspberries, strawberries, and cherries as bright as jewels.

The woman at the stall had smiled kindly. She had given him a cherry. It tasted as sweet as summer.

Ever since then, Paul had dreamed of cherries. He hoped and wished for cherries from the porridge pot.

He got up and crept down to the kitchen. The porridge pot stood on the stove. Paul tiptoed over the cold floor in his bare feet. He stretched up to hug the porridge pot.

"Please," he whispered. "Cherries. Cherries."

Paul was very small and the pot was very big. On tiptoe, on the cold floor, he wobbled. He lost his balance.

He fell, and the porridge pot tipped. It tumbled. And it smashed and crashed onto the floor!

Paul shut his eyes. He opened his mouth and screamed out a long, loud cry.

Curled up on the floor with the broken pieces of the pot, he cried and cried.

Everyone woke up and ran downstairs. Mrs. Molly put Paul on her knee and hugged him. He wanted to say he was very sorry, but he was crying too much.

"Paul!" said Mrs. Molly. "Look what happened!" Paul said nothing. He cried because he was hurt.

"Paul," said Mrs. Molly kindly. "Look!"

Paul dried his eyes. He looked. Nobody was mad at him. Everybody smiled.

On the floor there were four porridge pots.

One was full of hot buttery potatoes in their skins. One would not open at all. It had a label on it that said: *For Christmas Day and Paul's birthday.*

One was full of big yellow bananas and sunny oranges. Mrs. Molly took the lid off the last one.

It was full of bright red ...
"CHERRIES!" shouted Paul.
"Dark, plump, shiny cherries!" said Mrs. Molly.
"Yummy," said Jenny.
"They look like jewels," said Pippa.
"Ooh!" said Charlie.
"Thank you," said Paul.

More *Read-it!* Readers

Bright pictures and fun stories help you practice your reading skills. Look for more books at your level.

Dino Boulder Ball
Happy Birthday, Gus!
Happy Easter, Gus!
Happy Halloween, Gus!
Happy Thanksgiving, Gus!
Happy Valentine's Day, Gus!
Let's Go Fishing, Gus!
Make a New Friend, Gus!
Matt Goes to Mars
Merry Christmas, Gus!
Pick a Pet, Gus!
Rumble Meets Buddy Beaver
Rumble Meets Eli Elephant
Rumble Meets Penny Panther
Rumble Meets Wally Warthog
Rumble Meets Wilson Wolf
The Sand Witch
Terry Takes Off
Welcome to Third Grade, Gus!

Looking for a specific title or level? A complete list of *Read-it!* Readers is available on our Web site: **www.picturewindowbooks.com**